THE
STONEBOAT

For my children

To John and Nella with love

Groundwood Books / Douglas & McIntyre
585 Bloor Street West
Toronto, Ontario M6G 1K5

Distributed in the USA by Publishers Group West
1700 Fourth Street
Berkeley, CA 94710

We acknowledge the financial support of the Canada Council for the Arts, the Ontario Arts Council and the Government of Canada through the Book Publishing Industry Development Program for our publishing activities.

Canadian Cataloguing in Publication Data
Jam, Teddy
The stoneboat
1st ed.
"A Groundwood book".
ISBN 0-88899-368-4
I. Zhang, Ange. II. Title.
PS8569.A427S76 1999   jC813'.54   C99-930531-X
PZ7.J35St 1999

Design by Michael Solomon
Printed and bound in China by Everbest Printing Co. Ltd.

THE
STONEBOAT

TEDDY JAM

PICTURES BY
ANGE ZHANG

A GROUNDWOOD BOOK

DOUGLAS & McINTYRE VANCOUVER TORONTO BUFFALO

THE SPRING, when the melting snow makes Lion's Creek roar, is the time to go looking for catfish.

One Saturday after milking, my brother Evan and I went down with some fishing lines and a couple of buckets.

It was early morning. There were still patches of snow on the hills and the rising sun sent out a pink light that made those snow patches glow like wrapping paper.

Evan stood at the edge of the water wearing Dad's big boots, looking for fish to scoop up with his bucket.

I sat on the bank with my line. I used bread and a piece of bacon for bait.

After about fifteen minutes, when I hadn't caught anything, I walked up the creek a bit, around a corner where the water turned white as it foamed up the side of a big rock.

That was when I saw Mr. Richard, as my father called him. I found out later his name used to be pronounced Ree-shard, because sometime back before anyone but the schoolteacher's mother could remember, his family had been French. Back then, Mr. Richard's grandmother had been called Madame Ree-shard, and she would come to the school to teach French twice a week.

Mr. Richard was standing in the water like a big black-bearded statue wearing hip boots. He had a stained old fedora on his head, and a pitchfork in each hand poised above the roiling white water.

The sound of Lion's Creek was louder than a shout, so I said, "Hello, Mr. Ree-shard," because I knew he wouldn't hear me.

There was no place for me to put my line. The water was moving too fast. Just as I was about to turn back, I saw Mr. Richard stab one of his pitchforks down into the water. A second later it came up, a big silvery catfish writhing on its tines. He threw it onto the bank of the creek, then stabbed again. Over and over the big pitchforks slashed into the water. Again and again catfish were thrown wriggling onto the bank.

That spring Lion's Creek was huge. The water rushed through with a deafening roar, whirling and dancing as it smashed past rocks and logs. Sheets of icy spray were thrown up onto the bank where I stood watching Mr. Richard.

His beard was dripping and his mouth looked grim and sour. With each stab he stepped forward to meet the force of the water.

Suddenly he raised both pitchforks at once. With his black beard, his filthy hat, his giant arms spread out to kill, he looked like a vengeful horrible god preparing for a sacrifice.

Then he lost his footing and fell into the water.

His hat was swept away, and I could see his bare head, black hair plastered back from his white forehead. His head looked like a ball, a ball bouncing on the surface of the fast-moving water as he struggled to regain his balance.

"Evan," I screamed.

I saw Mr. Richard's head bounce against one of the rocks. Blood gushed out of the wound, and suddenly the white water was streaked with pink.

I was trying to get to him in the water, but I could only come close enough to stick my fishing rod out toward his hand. He pushed

it away and instead held out a pitchfork, handle first. I grabbed hold of it and was trying to use it to pull him up when I felt Evan's arms around my waist.

"Hang on or I'll kill you," Evan said. Then he yanked me back so hard that I thought my arms would come off.

"You know what?" my sister said that night. "You should have let Mr. Richard drown. We'd be a lot better off because Dad owes him two hundred dollars and doesn't know how he's ever going to pay it."

She was in the bedroom I shared with Evan. We hadn't told our parents what had happened at Lion's Creek. We were afraid that if we did, we wouldn't be allowed to go fishing.

"Two hundred dollars," I repeated. For only five hundred dollars the bank had made the Longleys sell their farm down the road. Evan and I went to the auction but left partway through. Afterwards the Longleys, on their way to live out west with Mrs. Longley's brother, brought us their cats.

Now I suddenly felt confused and sick to my stomach. Then I had an idea. "Well, he must think his own life is worth two hundred dollars," I said. "I saved it for him. He can't make Dad pay now."

But of course he could. Mr. Richard was his own law. He had the best land in the township and was famous for working it eighteen hours a day. He made more money than anyone else, then loaned it when others ran out of cash. Sometimes he could be seen standing in the parking lot at the church, collecting the weekly instalments everyone owed him in a big dark sock that bulged in his pocket all during service.

A week later, one Friday night when my parents had gone to a neighbor's for dinner, I snuck out after I was supposed to be in bed and walked past the barn toward the Richards' land.

I knew he'd be out there. Spring nights were perfect for removing the rocks that had heaved up into the fields during the winter. They would snag the plow if they weren't taken out before spring planting.

It wasn't so late. There was almost a full moon. It was halfway up the sky, shining so brightly that the trees made shadows. From far away I could hear the clinking of Mr. Richard's shovel and crowbar against the fieldstones. As I drew closer I could hear him grunting as he pulled out the rocks and threw them into the stoneboat, where they thudded into the wood bottom.

"I know my father owes you two hundred dollars," I was going to say to him. "But Evan and I saved your life..." That was as far as I had it worked out. I couldn't offer to work for him in the summer because my father needed us on our own farm. Maybe he would just see that my father was drowning in debt the way he had been drowning in the creek. Maybe he would reach in to help my father the way we had helped him. Or maybe he would just push his hat down on his head and pretend he hadn't heard me.

Even as I went up to him, Mr. Richard kept on working. With a long iron bar even taller than he was, he was trying to pry a huge boulder out of the ground.

When he had one edge free, I pushed the shovel underneath so it would stay raised. For a while we kept working around the boulder without talking. Each time he levered it higher, I would put a bar or a rock beneath. Finally it was raised enough that he could roll it away from its bed and onto the field.

There it lay, a giant pale egg in the moonlight, big enough to fill the crib my sister used to sleep in when she was a baby.

We stood beside it, panting and sweating. Mr. Richard had his sleeves rolled up. His arms were huge, even bigger than my father's. Down one was a long raised scar. Ever since I was little I'd known the story of how his house had burned down when he was a child, and his mother and two sisters had been killed.

I tried to gather my breath and my courage, finally ready to say my piece.

Mr. Richard pulled a pipe from his pocket. He sat down on the rock and began to stuff the pipe with tobacco. I sat down on the stoneboat.

Mr. Richard reached into his overalls again and pulled something out, tossed it toward me.

It was a large apple, getting soft the way spring apples do, but it would be my first apple in a month. I slowly wiped it clean on my shirt, then took a bite. Suddenly I remembered the Bible story about Adam taking a bite from the forbidden apple, and I had the terrible feeling that Mr. Richard had somehow tricked me.

"Thanks," he said. "You're a strong boy."

After we'd pulled him out of the river, Mr. Richard had sat on the bank for a long time, coughing water and trying to get his breath. The cut had stopped bleeding and he'd pulled his hat down to cover it. Then he'd stood up, gone behind a tree, brought up all the water that was still in his stomach and lungs.

"You boys go home now," he'd said. That was all.

Now he had taken off his hat and was sucking hard on his pipe. The burning tobacco glowed like a giant coal in the darkness, sending streaks of light up onto his face. I could see a big bandage wrapped around his head.

"When I finish this apple I'm going to talk," I said to myself. But as I got down to the core, Mr. Richard seemed so huge in the moonlight that every time I opened my mouth, it closed all by itself.

I put the core in my pocket, not sure Mr. Richard would like me throwing it into the field, the way I would have done at home. Maybe he saved his apple cores for his pigs, or took out all the seeds and tried to grow trees from them.

"I'll put this rock in," Mr. Richard said. "Then we'll dump everything on the fence."

He stood up from the rock, turned to face it, arched his back, then knelt before it like a weightlifter. He stretched out his arms, put one hand under either end, then with a grunt stood up, staggered forward a step, dumped the huge boulder into the stoneboat.

Mr. Richard was wiping his hands on his overalls when I saw my father crossing the field toward us. He was walking in a certain way I recognized, his arms swinging with each step. He must have come home and discovered my room empty.

"Strong boy," Mr. Richard said. "Knows how to lend a hand."

My father was on the other side of the stoneboat. He was surveying the load, the distance from the fence. It occurred to me my father might have come without even knowing I was there. Maybe he wanted to borrow more money. Or get more time to pay the other loan back.

Mr. Richard looked back and forth between us, as though he was curious to see what would happen. Then he stepped in front of the stoneboat, strapped himself into the leather harness and leaned into the weight.

The stoneboat had two long skids, like a sled. Once going, it would slide over the slick grass. But now Mr. Richard was bent almost down to the ground, huffing and panting as though he might explode.

I went to the back of the stoneboat to push. "Here it comes," my father said, joining me and lifting so hard that the skids of the stoneboat were freed from their ruts. With another grunt, Mr. Richard lurched forward and the boat began its slow creep across the field.

When we got to the fence, Mr. Richard unstrapped himself, then wiped the back of his hand across his mouth, as though he had just finished a meal.

The three of us positioned ourselves at the side of the boat. Later on my father said there must have been a ton of rocks, though of course that wouldn't have been possible.

The two men were sour with sweat. I was so tired from lifting and pushing I thought I must have hurt myself. Then I saw that Mr. Richard's cut had started bleeding again. The whole side of his face was covered with blood. He raised his hand and pushed at it, as though it were some kind of bug that would just fly away. I was too frightened to say anything.

"Now we push it over," he said, and without waiting for us he leaned into the stoneboat. I pushed as hard as I could while Mr. Richard and my father groaned and strained. Then suddenly Mr. Richard made a funny sound in his throat and the entire stoneboat rose in the air, almost fell back, then toppled upside down over the fence.

My father turned to me. "Guess you'd better go home now," he said.

I stood waiting for Mr. Richard to explain that in fact I was working for him, or had saved his life, or anything at all. But he just looked at me, as did my father. After a while I started walking. I was halfway across the field when I heard Mr. Richard say, "Thank you, neighbor."

When I got home, my mother was sitting on the front porch. If she knew where I had been, she didn't say. When my father arrived he kissed me, then lifted me up on his shoulder and carried me up to bed the way he used to when I was little.

"Everything is settled," was all he told me.

Years later Mr. Richard sold his farm and bought a small house on Lion's Creek, where it widens into a small lake. Once when I was at home for a visit I discovered that my father had become friends with him, and that they often went fishing together summer mornings.